The Little People of the Snow

by William Cullen Bryant

Copyright © 2/4/2016
Jefferson Publication

ISBN-13: 978-1523877843

Printed in the United States of America

THE LITTLE PEOPLE OF THE SNOW.

Alice.—One of your old-world stories, Uncle John,
Such as you tell us by the winter fire,
Till we all wonder it has grown so late.
Uncle John.—The story of the witch that ground to
death
Two children in her mill, or will you have
The tale of Goody Cutpurse?

Alice.—   Nay, now, nay;
Those stories are too childish, Uncle John,
Too childish even for little Willy here,
And I am older, two good years, than he;
No, let us have a tale of elves that ride,
By night, with jingling reins, or gnomes of the mine,
Or water-fairies, such as you know how

To spin, till Willy's eyes forget to wink,
And good Aunt Mary, busy as she is,
Lays down her knitting.

Uncle John.—   Listen to me, then.
'Twas in the olden time, long, long ago,
And long before the great oak at our door
Was yet an acorn, on a mountain's side

Lived, with his wife, a cottager. They dwelt
Beside a glen and near a dashing brook,
A pleasant spot in spring, where first the wren
Was heard to chatter, and, among the grass,
Flowers opened earliest; but, when winter came,
That little brook was fringed with other flowers,—
White flowers, with crystal leaf and stem, that grew
In clear November nights. And, later still,
That mountain glen was filled with drifted snows
From side to side, that one might walk across,
While, many a fathom deep, below, the brook
Sang to itself, and leaped and trotted on
Unfrozen, o'er its pebbles, toward the vale.

Alice.—A mountain's side, you said; the Alps, perhaps,
Or our own Alleghanies.
Uncle John.—   Not so fast,
My young geographer, for then the Alps,

With their broad pastures, haply were untrod
Of herdsman's foot, and never human voice
Had sounded in the woods that overhang
Our Alleghany's streams. I think it was
Upon the slopes of the great Caucasus,
Or where the rivulets of Ararat
Seek the Armenian vales. That mountain rose
So high, that, on its top, the winter snow
Was never melted, and the cottagers
Among the summer blossoms, far below,
Saw its white peaks in August from their door.
One little maiden, in that cottage home,
Dwelt with her parents, light of heart and limb,
Bright, restless, thoughtless, flitting here and there,

Like sunshine on the uneasy ocean waves,
And sometimes she forgot what she was bid,
As Alice does.

Alice.— Or Willy, quite as oft.
Uncle John.—But you are older, Alice, two good years,
And should be wiser. Eva was the name
Of this young maiden, now twelve summers old.
Now you must know that, in those early times,

When autumn days grew pale, there came a troop
Of childlike forms from that cold mountain top;
With trailing garments through the air they came,

Or walked the ground with girded loins, and threw
Spangles of silvery frost upon the grass,
And edged the brook with glistening parapets,

And built it crystal bridges, touched the pool,
And turned its face to glass, or, rising thence,
They shook, from their full laps, the soft, light snow,
And buried the great earth, as autumn winds
Bury the forest floor in heaps of leaves.

A beautiful race were they, with baby brows,
And fair, bright locks, and voices like the sound
Of steps on the crisp snow, in which they talked
With man, as friend with friend. A merry sight
It was, when, crowding round the traveller,
They smote him with their heaviest snow-flakes, flung
Needles of frost in handfuls at his cheeks,
And, of the light wreaths of his smoking breath,
Wove a white fringe for his brown beard, and laughed
Their slender laugh to see him wink and grin

And make grim faces as he floundered on.
But, when the spring came on, what terror reigned

Among these Little People of the Snow!
To them the sun's warm beams were shafts of fire,
And the soft south wind was the wind of death.
Away they flew, all with a pretty scowl
Upon their childish faces, to the north,
Or scampered upward to the mountain's top,
And there defied their enemy, the Spring;
Skipping and dancing on the frozen peaks,

And moulding little snow-balls in their palms,
And rolling them, to crush her flowers below,
Down the steep snow-fields.
Alice. —   That, too, must have been
A merry sight to look at.
Uncle John. —   You are right,
But I must speak of graver matters now.
Mid-winter was the time, and Eva stood,
Within the cottage, all prepared to dare
The outer cold, with ample furry robe
Close belted round her waist, and boots of fur,
And a broad kerchief, which her mother's hand
Had closely drawn about her ruddy cheek.

"Now, stay not long abroad," said the good dame,
"For sharp is the outer air, and, mark me well,
Go not upon the snow beyond the spot
Where the great linden bounds the neighboring field."
The little maiden promised, and went forth,
And climbed the rounded snow-swells firm with frost
Beneath her feet, and slid, with balancing arms,

Into the hollows. Once, as up a drift
She slowly rose, before her, in the way,
She saw a little creature lily-cheeked,
With flowing flaxen locks, and faint blue eyes,
That gleamed like ice, and robe that only seemed
Of a more shadowy whiteness than her cheek.
On a smooth bank she sat.

Alice.—   She must have been
One of your Little People of the Snow.
Uncle John.—She was so, and, as Eva now drew near
The tiny creature bounded from her seat;
"And come," she said, "my pretty friend; to-day
We will be playmates. I have watched thee long,
And seen how well thou lov'st to walk these drifts,
And scoop their fair sides into little cells,
And carve them with quaint figures, huge-limbed men,
Lions, and griffins. We will have, to-day,
A merry ramble over these bright fields,
And thou shalt see what thou hast never seen."
On went the pair, until they reached the bound

Where the great linden stood, set deep in snow,
Up to the lower branches. "Here we stop,"
Said Eva, "for my mother has my word
That I will go no further than this tree."
Then the snow-maiden laughed: "And what is this?
This fear of the pure snow, the innocent snow,
That never harmed aught living? Thou mayst roam
For leagues beyond this garden, and return
In safety; here the grim wolf never prowls,
And here the eagle of our mountain-crags
Preys not in winter. I will show the way
And bring thee safely home. Thy mother, sure,
Counselled thee thus because thou hadst no guide."
By such smooth words was Eva won to break
Her promise, and went on with her new friend,
Over the glistening snow and down a bank
Where a white shelf, wrought by the eddying wind,

Like to a billow's crest in the great sea,
Curtained an opening. "Look, we enter here."
And straight, beneath the fair o'erhanging fold,
Entered the little pair that hill of snow,

Walking along a passage with white walls,
And a white vault above where snow-stars shed
A wintry twilight. Eva moved in awe,

And held her peace, but the snow-maiden smiled,
And talked and tripped along, as, down the way,
Deeper they went into that mountainous drift.
And now the white walls widened, and the vault
Swelled upward, like some vast cathedral dome,
Such as the Florentine, who bore the name
Of heaven's most potent angel, reared, long since,
Or the unknown builder of that wondrous fane,
The glory of Burgos. Here a garden lay,
In which the Little People of the Snow
Were wont to take their pastime when their tasks
Upon the mountain's side and in the clouds
Were ended. Here they taught the silent frost
To mock, in stem and spray, and leaf and flower,

The growths of summer. Here the palm upreared
Its white columnar trunk and spotless sheaf
Of plume-like leaves; here cedars, huge as those

Of Lebanon, stretched far their level boughs,
Yet pale and shadowless; the sturdy oak
Stood, with its huge gnarled roots of seeming strength,
 Fast anchored, in the glistening bank; light sprays
Of myrtle, roses in their bud and bloom,
Drooped by the winding walks; yet all seemed wrought
Of stainless alabaster; up the trees
Ran the lithe jessamine, with stalk and leaf
Colorless as her flowers. "Go softly on,"
Said the snow-maiden; "touch not, with thy hand,
The frail creation round thee, and beware

To sweep it with thy skirts. Now look above.
How sumptuously these bowers are lighted up
With shifting gleams that softly come and go!
These are the northern lights, such as thou seest
In the midwinter nights, cold, wandering flames,
That float, with our processions, through the air;
And here, within our winter palaces,
Mimic the glorious daybreak." Then she told
How, when the wind, in the long winter nights,
Swept the light snows into the hollow dell,
She and her comrades guided to its place
Each wandering flake, and piled them quaintly up,
In shapely colonnade and glistening arch,
With shadowy aisles between, or bade them grow

Beneath their little hands, to bowery walks
In gardens such as these, and, o'er them all,
Built the broad roof. "But thou hast yet to see
A fairer sight," she said, and led the way
To where a window of pellucid ice
Stood in the wall of snow, beside their path.
"Look, but thou mayst not enter." Eva looked,

And lo! a glorious hall, from whose high vault
Stripes of soft light, ruddy, and delicate green,
And tender blue, flowed downward to the floor
And far around, as if the aerial hosts,
That march on high by night, with beamy spears,
And streaming banners, to that place had brought
Their radiant flags to grace a festival.

And in all that hall a joyous multitude
Of those by whom its glistening walls were reared,
Whirled in a merry dance to silvery sounds,
That rang from cymbals of transparent ice,
And ice-cups, quivering to the skilful touch
Of little fingers. Round and round they flew,
As when, in spring, about a chimney-top,

A cloud of twittering swallows, just returned,
Wheel round and round, and turn and wheel again,
Unwinding their swift track. So rapidly
Flowed the meandering stream of that fair dance,
Beneath that dome of light. Bright eyes that looked
From under lily brows, and gauzy scarfs

Sparkling like snow-wreaths in the early sun,
Shot by the window in their mazy whirl.

And there stood Eva, wondering at the sight
Of those bright revellers and that graceful sweep
Of motion as they passed her;—long she gazed,
And listened long to the sweet sounds that thrilled
The frosty air, till now the encroaching cold
Recalled her to herself. "Too long, too long
I linger here," she said, and then she sprang
Into the path, and with a hurried step
Followed it upward. Ever by her side
Her little guide kept pace. As on they went
Eva bemoaned her fault: "What must they think—
The dear ones in the cottage, while so long,
Hour after hour, I stay without? I know
That they will seek me far and near, and weep
To find me not. How could I, wickedly,
Neglect the charge they gave me?" As she spoke,

The hot tears started to her eyes; she knelt
In the mid path. "Father! forgive this sin;
Forgive myself I cannot"—thus she prayed,
 And rose and hastened onward. When, at last,
They reached the outer air, the clear north breathed
A bitter cold, from which she shrank with dread,
But the snow-maiden bounded as she felt
The cutting blast, and uttered shouts of joy,

And skipped, with boundless glee, from drift to drift,
And danced round Eva, as she labored up
The mounds of snow, "Ah me! I feel my eyes
Grow heavy," Eva said; "they swim with sleep;
I cannot walk for utter weariness,
And I must rest a moment on this bank,
But let it not be long." As thus she spoke,
In half-formed words, she sank on the smooth snow,
With closing lids. Her guide composed the robe
About her limbs, and said, "A pleasant spot

Is this to slumber in; on such a couch
Oft have I slept away the winter night,

And had the sweetest dreams." So Eva slept,
But slept in death; for when the power of frost
Locks up the motions of the living frame,
The victim passes to the realm of Death
Through the dim porch of Sleep. The little guide,
Watching beside her, saw the hues of life
Fade from the fair smooth brow and rounded cheek,
As fades the crimson from a morning cloud,
Till they were white as marble, and the breath
Had ceased to come and go, yet knew she not
At first that this was death. But when she marked
How deep the paleness was, how motionless
That once lithe form, a fear came over her.
She strove to wake the sleeper, plucked her robe,
And shouted in her ear, but all in vain;
The life had passed away from those young limbs.

Then the snow-maiden raised a wailing cry,
Such as a dweller in some lonely wild,
Sleepless through all the long December night,
Hears when the mournful East begins to blow.

But suddenly was heard the sound of steps,
Grating on the crisp snow; the cottagers

Were seeking Eva; from afar they saw
The twain, and hurried toward them. As they came,
With gentle chidings ready on their lips,
And marked that death-like sleep, and heard the tale
Of the snow-maiden, mortal anguish fell
Upon their hearts, and bitter words of grief
And blame were uttered: "Cruel, cruel one,
To tempt our daughter thus, and cruel we,
Who suffered her to wander forth alone
In this fierce cold." They lifted the dear child,
And bore her home and chafed her tender limbs,

And strove, by all the simple arts they knew,
To make the chilled blood move, and win the breath
Back to her bosom; fruitlessly they strove.
The little maid was dead. In blank despair
They stood, and gazed at her who never more

Should look on them. "Why die we not with her?"
They said; "without her life is bitterness."

Now came the funeral day; the simple folk
Of all that pastoral region gathered round,
To share the sorrow of the cottagers.
They carved a way into the mound of snow
To the glen's side, and dug a little grave
In the smooth slope, and, following the bier,
In long procession from the silent door,
Chanted a sad and solemn melody.

"Lay her away to rest within the ground.
Yea, lay her down whose pure and innocent life
Was spotless as these snows; for she was reared
In love, and passed in love life's pleasant spring,
And all that now our tenderest love can do
Is to give burial to her lifeless limbs."
They paused. A thousand slender voices round,
Like echoes softly flung from rock and hill,
Took up the strain, and all the hollow air
Seemed mourning for the dead; for, on that day,
The little people of the snow had come,

From mountain-peak, and cloud, and icy hall,
To Eva's burial. As the murmur died,
The funeral train renewed the solemn chant.
"Thou, Lord, hast taken her to be with Eve,
Whose gentle name was given her. Even so,
For so Thy wisdom saw that it was best
For her and us. We bring our bleeding hearts,
And ask the touch of healing from Thy hand,
As, with submissive tears, we render back
The lovely and beloved to Him who gave."

They ceased. Again the plaintive murmur rose.
From shadowy skirts of low-hung cloud it came,
And wide white fields, and fir-trees capped with snow,
Shivering to the sad sounds. They sank away
To silence in the dim-seen distant woods.
The little grave was closed; the funeral train
Departed; winter wore away; the spring

Steeped, with her quickening rains, the violet tufts,
By fond hands planted where the maiden slept.
But, after Eva's burial, never more
The Little People of the Snow were seen
By human eye, nor ever human ear
Heard from their lips, articulate speech again;
For a decree went forth to cut them off,
Forever, from communion with mankind.

The winter clouds, along the mountain-side,
Rolled downward toward the vale, but no fair form
Leaned from their folds, and, in the icy glens,
And aged woods, under snow-loaded pines,
Where once they made their haunt, was emptiness.

But ever, when the wintry days drew near,
Around that little grave, in the long night,
Frost-wreaths were laid and tufts of silvery rime
In shape like blades and blossoms of the field,
As one would scatter flowers upon a bier.

www.ingramcontent.com/pod-product-compliance
Lightning Source LLC
Chambersburg PA
CBHW061443050726
47593CB00004B/1451